The Red Path
(Fear)

By Nima Sheikhy

Illustrated by Nilo Rouse

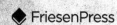 FriesenPress

One Printers Way
Altona, MB R0G 0B0
Canada

www.friesenpress.com

ISBN
978-1-03-913813-1 (Hardcover)
978-1-03-913812-4 (Paperback)
978-1-03-913814-8 (eBook)

1. JUVENILE FICTION, SOCIAL ISSUES, EMOTIONS & FEELINGS

Distributed to the trade by The Ingram Book Company

Introduction

According to Merriam-Webster, fear is defined as "an unpleasant often strong emotion caused by anticipation or awareness of danger."

Experiencing this emotion may be unpleasant, but it is the main element of survival. Our mind recognizes threats and aims to protect the self. Picture this: crossing a busy street, a speeding car coming in your direction. The instant reaction to get away is triggered by fear. It is there to serve and protect.

There are also moments that our mind misleads us to believe there is a threat. For example, the first day of school, the fifth-grade exam, choosing the outfit for the first day of high school, the job interview, the project that is due next week … Our mind may create a gigantic scary picture of something that in reality may be otherwise. In all these cases, there is a deadline, so we have to face them, no matter how. Once they are done, we realize that they were not as scary as we thought. Chances are the process may even have been a bit pleasant.

We also have wishes, thoughts, ideas, and dreams with no deadline. Our mind creates a gigantic scary image of the path that we must go through. Therefore, we wait for the perfect moment for days, months, years, and maybe decades.

Let me flash back a bit and share how we got here.

Donya, my four-year-old daughter, and I had a bedtime story routine. I made up stories filled with animal characters going through events and incidents, which came to some sort of conclusion to teach her something. One night, I came home and found her awake in her room. She did not want to go to bed because she was afraid of the dark. I decided to tell her a story about a cat who was afraid of the dark. As I started the intro, she interrupted me.

"Daddy ... please tell me an exciting story. I don't like those long speechy ones."

She was looking at me with the most adorable eyes, waiting to hear an exciting story. A tale came to mind about a mysterious path, which leads one to recognize the nature of fear, to learn about the rules and exceptions of this world. I called it "The Red Path." She listened to my raw story and loved it.

A few years later my son, Daniel, came into this world. These two creatures have the purest of minds and the most innocent souls. They are my main source of encouragement to move forward. As the kids were growing up, I observed their fascination with tales and noticed that they could understand any message as long as it was in the context of a story.

When Donya was eight years old and Daniel was two, my marriage came to an end. It was a painful journey for all of us as a family. Life was happening along with the love of finishing the book. This long road, with all its ups and downs, and overcoming once so scary challenges, helped me face my own fears, which turned into more symbolic ideas for the story. It was a decade-long journey of rewriting it more than thirty times. Once I knew in my heart I was done with the content, I took the first step toward publishing, and there were a thousand little steps to follow. Each step showed me my own fear of taking the next one.

"The Red Path" is the first book of seven. Our journey will extend into anger, wonder, sadness, love, oneness, and happiness.

I dedicate this book to Donya and Daniel, who were the cause and the journey-mates. The characters of Hoorad and Hirad were based on Donya and Daniel. The characters of King Nate and Queen Maya were inspired by King Solomon and Queen Belqis in Rumi's stories.

Special thanks to Dr. Parviz Sahabi, for sharing his wisdom in his Rumi classes at the Zavieh Mystical Study Center. Donya Sheikhy and Sonnet Kazemnia for content editing, Nilo Rouse for her magical illustration design, and Mozhgan Kermanshahy for her exceptional layout design.

Enjoy your moments.

Nima Sheikhy

Chapter 1

The Curiosity

Thousands of years ago, hidden deep in the heart of a humble forest, nestled in a beautiful castle, lived King Nate and his wife Maya. Together they ruled the land and had two captivating children, Hooda and Hirad.

The castle was surrounded by many mysterious paths and strange animals. Life there was exceedingly interesting. Each day, breakfast was served inside the castle. The children would later have their lunch in the courtyard surrounded by extraordinary violet flowers. Finally, dinner was served under the moonlight, nestled in a corner behind the tall willow trees.

The curious-eyed, seven-year-old girl Hooda loved adventures. Hirad, the four-year-old boy, was playful, sweet, and talkative. One could often find him playing outside with the dogs and squirrels. Hirad loved running around all day more than anything; Hooda, on the other hand, was more into exploring and discovering. You would find Hirad jumping from one tree to another while Hooda was curiously observing the color of a butterfly's wings.

The children had a favorite pet, Misha, who always accompanied them on their many quests in the forest. They had a special bond with one another and lived a very harmonious life together.

King Nate had extraordinary abilities. The King was not only able to speak to animals, but had a mission to spread inner peace, hope, and love to all. Like other kings, Nate needed assistants to run his kingdom, but Nate's aid came from an unusual place: the prominent animal kingdom.

The citizens of Nate's land were all animals. For the kingdom to remain strong and to keep its balance, every animal had a specific task assigned to them.

These tasks were decided based on their strengths. Ellie, the elephant, used her powerful snout to grab water and wash the pathway clean. She would also help lift heavy packages when Nate requested it.

The family of little squirrels oversaw the gathering of different kinds of nuts and brought them to the castle for royal meals. Jenny, the giraffe, used her tall neck to dust and clean places that no one else could reach. Missy the Mouse and Kati the Cat were playful, you know. They kept the kingdom magical and helped it thrive in joy and beauty.

While every single animal was special, there was one that stood above them all: the marvellous lapwing. Her special ability was to sense any coming danger, even from miles away. She was the protector of the entire kingdom. No matter what situation arose, she would appear right on time and become the saving angel. That is precisely why King Nate named her "Angel."

There was one more thing that made the family's life even more magical: the flying carpet. Nate had a magical carpet which, upon his—and only his—command, would take anybody anywhere in the world. Nate usually used it for family vacation to far-away places. You see, thousands of years ago there were no airplanes, and the flying carpet acted as their private jet.

During the day, Hooda and Hirad loved walking around the castle with Nate. They were mesmerized by the way King Nate spoke. As the King explained the ways of the world, the children were captivated by his leadership. He always maintained a calm voice, which allowed their imaginations to fly. King Nate would explain the rules to his children, and how there were always exceptions to those rules.

Often Hooda was inspired by her father's philosophical talks, but occasionally, she would get bored of King Nate's long speeches. One day, while walking around the castle, Hooda noticed a trail far away from the castle.

"Daddy, what is that?" Hooda asked.

"I have named it red path," Nate said. "It is covered by tall red rosebushes. Do not worry your mind about that right now. One day, you will go down that path. There is something there that you need to experience. Wait one more year, then I shall take you there."

"Daddy, what do you mean?" Hooda asked. "Experience what? Can we go now? Why must I wait for one more year?"

In his soft tone, Nate said, "My princess, every stage of life is supposed to come at a certain age; every step that you take should be age-appropriate for you. It is not good for you to experience the red path now; just wait a year and we will go through it together. Some paths in life you cannot go alone, you need to have a leader or some sort of guidance. I will guide you all the way through, I promise."

"Daddy," Hooda asked curiously. "I don't understand what you're saying, experience what? What was that word? Age-appropriate? What does that mean? You're confusing me."

"Age-appropriate means that you are old enough to experience certain things," the King said. "Red path is not something that I can explain, you need to experience it for yourself when you are old enough. It is only a year. Be patient, you can do it."

"You're killing me," Hooda replied.

"Well, my daughter, that is not my intention. I am just protecting you."

"Ahhhhh, I am dying to see what the red path is about." Hooda bit her lips nervously.

Nate chuckled. "You will, my love, you will soon. Just be patient. You see, patience is an art, and it only comes with practice; it makes things more intriguing. Here is your chance to practice and be grateful for this opportunity."

Hooda started to mimic her dad, mumbling under her breath with high tones and a scrunched-up face. "Here is your chance to practice, be grateful to the opportunity."

"Did you say something?" her father asked.

"No Daddy, I was just practicing patience."

They both laughed.

Nate put his strong arms around Hooda. "I love you, my princess. Let's go and enjoy our day."

Besides exploring around with her little brother all day, Hooda had a routine of walking around the castle after lunch all by herself and exploring nature. She usually passed by her little brother, giving him a gentle kiss on his forehead, then proceeded to pet Misha, who was taking a nap under the warm afternoon sun. She later headed outside for a relaxing walk.

One day after lunch she went for her regular walk around the castle. She had been starring at the red path from a distance for a while and was curious to know what the big deal was. After the discussion with her father, she was even more curious.

That afternoon she came out, looked at the path, and could not help herself. She began to walk towards it. As she was getting closer, Hooda noticed that the bushes were far bigger than they had appeared from a distance. She glanced at the castle for a moment with doubt. The castle looked much smaller than it was; letting go of that familiar scenery was hard.

She stood there for a few seconds, looked around, then walked up to the path. Her heart was pounding. The path, which was lined by gigantic red rosebushes, was intimidating. She took a deep breath and began to walk down it. As she went in further and deeper, the bushes got bigger and taller, until it was hard to see anything around them. She reached a point where the top of the bushes came together and created a dark, chilling tunnel where there were absolutely no lights from any source. Frightened, Hooda started to run farther along the path. She tripped over something and fell to the ground; looking down, she saw a giant snake lying across the path behind her.

Terrified now, Hooda ran faster than ever before. Suddenly, she saw a very narrow sliver of light appear down the rose tunnel and ran towards it. She followed the light and found her way out.

As soon as Hooda caught her breath, she noticed an ocean in the far distance. In the distant waves, sharks jumped up and down attacked each other. On the shore, a bunch of crocodiles crawled around and attacked everything that surrounded them. On the sand, creepy giant crabs crawled on top of each other.

Hooda was petrified and started to cry as loud and as hard as she could. She screamed, "Somebody, somebody please save me from this nightmare! I can't take it anymore!"

Angel, the brave gigantic lapwing, showed up and landed right beside her "I sensed that you were in trouble, so I came immediately. What is wrong, my dear?"

She cried and said, "Please just take me to my dad, Angel."

"Not a problem. Hop on my back and I will take you to him."

Angel flew as fast as she possibly could and took Hooda back to her father. The pair landed in the garden, where Nate was waiting for them. Hooda hopped off and ran toward him, crying. "I'm sorry I didn't listen to you. I never want to go back there, ever!!"

"You are safe, my dear. I am sorry too, for making you curious and confused."

"Please carry me. I can't walk anymore."

Nate picked her up and kissed her forehead several times. "Don't worry, my princess. You are safe now."

Hooda was still crying on her father's powerful shoulders. "Daddy, I'm so scared. I'm frightened, and I never want to go back there. You have no idea how horrible it was. I shouldn't have gone there. I am so, so sorry."

"It's okay my love... Don't worry."

Hearing all the noise, Queen Maya had come to the garden to investigate. When she saw her daughter, she hugged her tight. "My poor little girl. You are becoming a big girl; remember that it's okay to be scared. You are safe now; we all love you so much. Look at those adorable eyes!"

Misha was licking her legs, and between that and her mother's soothing words, Hooda started to giggle and laugh.

Maya took her inside and rubbed aloe vera leaves on the scrapes she had gotten when she fell. Maya held Hooda in her loving arms. One of the squirrels brought special nuts and a cheese sandwich.

While she was eating, Nate started to talk in his famous philosophical tone. "My princess, curiosity and confusion are like the twin shadows of each other. When curiosity appears, confusion follows. The confusion brings more curiosity, and more curiosity creates more confusion. These two play their game until fear shows up, the fear of the unknown. You were curious, confused, and fearful. That is quite normal."

Hooda fell asleep while Nate talking, and Maya gently carried her to bed. The king and queen stood there watching their princess in a very deep sleep. King Nate whispered, "My princess, tomorrow is a new chapter in your life."

Chapter 2

The Experience

Right at dawn the next day, Nate woke Hooda.

"Why are you waking me up so early?" she asked.

"Because we have things to do today," he told her. He gestured to the table, where a simple breakfast was laid out.

With her endearing eyes looking up at him with trust, Hooda got out of bed and went to the table, "What things?"

"You will find out. Finish your breakfast first."

"But I don't feel hungry."

"Have a small bite."

Hooda started to eat a little bit. When she had finished a few bites, she asked, "So, do you want to tell me what's going on?"

"You will find out soon. Grab the backpack," Nate said calmly.

Hooda looked around the room and spotted a backpack. When she went to get it and looked inside, she saw it was full of goodies including water, snacks, juice, blankets, a lantern, and many other items one would take on a camping trip.

"What's going on? What do I need these for?"

"Just please follow me," the King said in his royal voice.

Father and daughter walked out of the main doors of the castle together, and into the courtyard leading away from the castle. Nate had started walking toward the red path when suddenly Hooda froze.

"Daddy, are we going toward the red path? I told you that I don't ever want to go back there, not ever!"

"Hooda, do you trust me?" the King asked very sternly.

She said she did, but her voice betrayed her deep uncertainty.

"Then follow me. I will protect you no matter what."

Hooda did not move. Instead, she widened her big brown eyes, raised her eyebrows, and yelled, "But Daddy, there were sharks! And crocodiles! Why should I go back there? I don't want to. Please don't force me!"

The King took a minute to think, and said, "You are aware that I speak the animal language. There is no reason for you to be scared. You have me here, and I will protect you no matter what. I promise you, trust me."

Nervously, Hooda agreed; she started to walk with heavy steps toward the red path.

When they got to its beginning, Hooda stopped again. "Daddy. I do not want to go any farther. You have no idea what lives in there! The bushes get so tall that even Jenny the giraffe couldn't stand a chance of seeing over them! Not only that, but there are animals I bet even Angel couldn't beat! And Daddy! Most importantly, it gets so dark and narrow that not even a lantern could light your way. Why are you forcing me to do this? I don't want to come. I'm done, I'm going home."

"My darling, I have been down this path several times. I can close my eyes and walk through it without missing a step," the King said calmly. "Please," he added, now a little sterner. "Trust me. I will guide you all the way through."

Hooda did not say a word. She kept quiet and looked at the ground.

The King paused for a moment, as he knew very well Hooda was not convinced. "I know I am repeating myself," Nate said, "but I feel like you must hear it again. Please remember I know how to speak to animals, and once I start speaking their language, they will not harm you. Will you trust me?"

"I don't know, I guess?"

Nate grabbed his daughter's hand and they started to move. As they walked further and further along the path, they reached the point where it became totally dark. Hooda stopped for the third time and started to beg her father to go back.

"Daddy, I can't take it anymore, it's dark, I can't see anything. I'm petrified, please don't make me go any farther."

"My princess, please take five deep breaths."

"What?"

"Just take five deep breaths."

Hooda, with a confused voice, said, "Okay? One … two … three … four … five."

"Now, look around and tell me what you see."

Hooda stopped and looked away. Amazed, she observed that after a few seconds she was starting to see in the dark. "Daddy! I can see a little bit." She had a bit more cheer in her voice. "How come?"

"My dear, whenever life gets scary, just take five deep breaths, wait a bit, and then you can see things more clearly. Now go on, tell me. What else do you see?"

"Umm, I see branches, rosebushes, grass, and some flying birds." Now her voice held more confidence.

"Hmmm," the King said, "so what you are telling me is that even when you think you cannot see anything, and you know you are surrounded by total darkness…if you wait a little bit, you will be able to see?"

"Yeah, I guess?"

Nate kneeled down next to Hooda and put his arms around her. "Now I want you to look at the ground and tell me what you see."

Hooda did so and started to scream. "The snake is here! The snake is here!" she yelled as her heart pounded. "Oh my god, Daddy, save me! Please, Daddy! Daddy, talk to it, talk to it!"

Totally calm, Nate gave his daughter a wide smile.

"What are you smiling at?" Hooda asked. "There's a snake on the ground! Save me!"

"Please pick it up," Nate said.

Hooda was horrified. "Why would I do that??"

Nate sighed. "Remember my words, my sweet child? I can talk to animals. Trust me. Grab it."

Hooda's heart was pounding. She bent over and reached for the snake with a shaky hand, grabbed it, and brought it up to eye level. But to her surprise she saw that she was not holding a snake at all; she was holding a big, twisty tree branch.

Hooda was shocked and amazed. "But Daddy, it was like a snake!"

Nate smiled. "Hmmm, things are not always what they seem to be. You just have to have the courage to get to know them, right?"

Hooda held the twisty branch, her eyes filled with wonder, and nodded.

"Now," Nate instructed, "I want you to hold the branch above your head."

Hooda raised the branch above her head as she was told. It was heavy and big, but she managed.

As her hands were getting high above her head, suddenly everything brightened. She looked up and saw that the branch was tall enough to push open the bushes. She was amazed and looked at her father, wondering how things were changing.

Nate had a huge grin through his beard. "Hooda, whenever in life you feel petrified, surrounded by total darkness, wait for a while. Take five deep breaths and look around. All the tools you need to light up the path are there; you just need to have the courage to use them. That is the rule of life."

Hooda smiled at her father, victorious and admiring.

"Now," Nate said as he looked at Hooda, "I ask you to lead our way with your magic branch."

Hooda started to walk in front of the King, using her branch to open the bushes. The path was not so scary anymore; there were lights and hope.

As Hooda was walking and lighting up the path, King Nate followed her and sang with his heavenly voice: "There is a crack, a crack in everything. That's how the light gets in."

As they reached the other end of the path, Hooda suddenly stopped. She remembered that this was where she had seen all the scary animals.

"Okay," Hooda said nervously. "This is where we stop. I've seen enough. I've experienced enough, please don't make me. Please, please, please, let us go back home!"

"Now please," Nate said as he looked at his daughter, "stand here and take five deep breaths."

"Okay, Daddy. One … two … three … four … five."

Hooda waited for a moment and looked at the scenery in distance. "I'm still seeing the sharks, crocodiles, and all those creepy animals. Nothing is going to change, I've seen enough, let's go back."

Nate looked at his daughter. "Do you trust me?"

"Yes, of course I do, why do you keep asking me that?"

"Because I see the fear in your eyes," the King said softly. "I am just trying to remind you that you are safe with me. At this point, my princess, rest, have a sip of water, eat some snacks, and then we will move toward the ocean. I promise to protect you. None of those animals will ever be able to harm you. The only thing I ask of you is to keep your head down. I will guide you every step of the way."

"But…but…but…"

"No buts." Nate made a space for Hooda to sit. "Sit down, eat your snack, and when you are ready, we will go."

"Okay, Daddy."

After their short break, they embarked on their journey again. Hooda kept her head down, deep in her thoughts, thinking of how she could protect herself against the sharks and crocodiles.

They walked for a long time.

Nate's voice brought her back to reality. "Now, I ask you to look up and see."

Hooda looked up. To her surprise, there was no ocean of any kind; instead, there was a lake. There were no sharks, there were only cute little goldfish. There were no crocodiles, there were only playful, multicolored lizards. Finally, there were no gigantic crabs, there were only black, fluffy baby spiders running around and playing.

Hooda looked at her dad, confused. "But…but I saw the ocean! Sharks, crocodiles, crabs. Where are they? What's happening?"

Nate smiled. "You know that I am fascinated by rules and exceptions. Everything in this world is little when you look at it from afar, and much bigger when you get closer, right? That is the rule. But fear is the exception. Your fears seem so big from a distance, and so little when you face them. This mysterious path is called the red path because red is the color of fear. When you are afraid, your concerns look a lot bigger from a distance. When you get closer, everything changes. The human mind generates thoughts and plays games; sometimes, it gets overprotective and makes a big deal of little things. Always remember, my dear princess, that to beat the game of fear, you just need to follow the five-deep-breath routine. Once you're done counting, look around. This will help you see things more clearly and recognize your tools. Remember when you saw everything so gigantic and big from distance?"

"Yes," Hooda said, a little embarrassed.

"Well, when you got the courage to move toward the fearful scenery, you found out that everything was not as it seemed."

"Yes," Hooda said excitedly. "Instead of the ocean, I now see a lake. Instead of the shark, I now recognize the bright goldfish." She paused, amazed at what she just learned. "Daddy, I love you," Hooda said as she wrapped her arm around Nate.

There was a moment of silence.

That evening, Hooda and Nate sat beside the lake and enjoyed the sunset. They ate the apples and sandwiches packed with them and enjoyed the moment together.

Nate turned his head toward Hooda. "You see how beautiful this is? How much we are enjoying each other's company in this once-scary place? If we had not overcome our fear, we would not have had this moment. Thank you for being a wonderful journey-mate. I am proud of you, and I love you."

"I love you too, Daddy," Hooda said, "but I have a question. How come last year you brought a bunch of red roses for your anniversary with mum, and when I asked why red roses, you said they were the symbol of love? How is that possible? Is red the symbol of fear or love?"

Nate thought for a moment. "Fear and love are like twin sisters. If you do not overcome your fear, you will never fall in love."

"So, you were scared when you first saw Mommy?"

Nate chuckled. "Yes and no, dear. I was excited to see your Mummy—I could not take my eyes off her—but at the same time, I feared my feelings. Eventually I overcame my fears and talked to her." The King went on. "When I say love, I do not only talk about the love for other people. You may have a love for your goals, dreams, and desires, but feel scared to go toward them. Only once you are ready will you go towards them. My princess, fear and love will always come together. Always remember curiosity comes first, which makes you go after something, and then confusion will follow, along with fear. Once all this happens, only then will love to appear."

"So, when I got curious and then afraid, that was when I was able to see the reality of the scary path?"

"Exactly," the King said, proud of his daughter. "Only then did you feel joy." He paused. "There is a path far, far, far away from the castle called green path or, as I call it, the happiness path. Your Mummy and I went on that path for our first date."

"Really?" Hooda asked, intrigued. "Can you take me there next? Pleeeease?" She made her lips into a pout.

Nate smiled at his daughter's charm. "There are five more paths you need to go through before you will be ready for the green path. The next path is anger, the purple path. Then Wonder, Sadness, Love, Oneness, and finally Happiness."

"I can't wait to experience those with you," Hooda said, excited about their next adventure.

"We will do the purple path next year," the King said as he looked at his daughter with a smile. "And we will bring Mommy, Hirad, and Misha with us."

"I can't wait to go back home and share my experience with Mummy and Hirad!"

"You will, my dear, but for now, just look at the beautiful scenery, celebrate your victory, and enjoy your moment."

The End

"There is a crack, a crack in everything.
That's how the light gets in."
Taken from Leonard Cohen's song "Anthem"

Lightning Source UK Ltd.
Milton Keynes UK
UKHW020158131222
413812UK00003B/101